the ADVENTURES of SHADOWMAN

by Tom Listul

illustrated by Jenna Douglas

Order this book online at www.trafford.com
or email orders@trafford.com

Most Trafford titles are also available at major online book retailers.

Trafford PUBLISHING® www.trafford.com

North America & international
toll-free: 844 688 6899 (USA & Canada)
fax: 812 355 4082

Our mission is to efficiently provide the world's finest, most comprehensive book publishing service, enabling every author to experience success. To find out how to publish your book, your way, and have it available worldwide, visit us online at www.trafford.com

Because of the dynamic nature of the Internet, any web addresses or links contained in this book may have changed since publication and may no longer be valid. The views expressed in this work are solely those of the author and do not necessarily reflect the views of the publisher, and the publisher hereby disclaims any responsibility for them.

Any people depicted in stock imagery provided by Getty Images are models, and such images are being used for illustrative purposes only.
Certain stock imagery © Getty Images.

ISBN: 978-1-4907-9932-2 (sc)
ISBN: 978-1-4907-9933-9 (e)

Library of Congress Control Number: 2023900580

Print information available on the last page.

Trafford rev. 01/10/2023

I have a story to tell you;
it's all **amazing** and really really true.
I know you won't believe me, but just read on
and you will see.
Maybe it could even happen to you!

There is a man who lives on
our bedroom wall.
I don't understand it, and I
can't explain it.
Each night I wonder if he will come
out when we call.

As my brother and I
crawl into our beds,
and a chapter from
our favorite book is being read,
out of the shadows,
against the nightlight,
Shadowman appears just to say
"Goodnight".

With a voice so low and
gurgly and gravelly.
When first Shadowman starts
to talk, I'm kind of glad my dad
is right there next to me.

But soon he is not scary at all as he
takes shape on the wall
stretching and bending
in every which way.

He can make his face **long**, and his chin stick out.

Or he can **scrunch** down tight and begin to **pout**.

He can make his hair stand **straight up** on top of his head.

Sometimes his hair looks **scrunched and silly** like he just got out of bed.

Shadowman tells stories of **princesses and castles**
and playing in a forest with all kinds of **animals.**

Sometimes his stories make me laugh so hard my legs start to kick. And I **wiggle and giggle** as I watch each one of his tricks.

Dad sits on the bed not saying a word

As Shadowman tells **adventures**
that I have never heard.

"Time for bed," we hear my dad say as he
turns down the light.
As Shadowman disappears once again into the dark,
we wave goodbye and tell him,
"I love you, sweet dreams and goodnight."

Printed in the United States
by Baker & Taylor Publisher Services